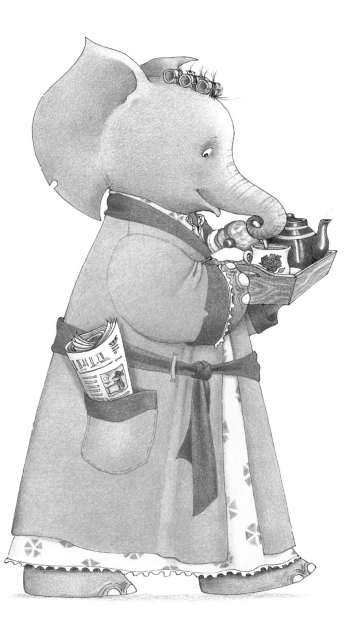

Five Minutes' Peace

— and —

All In One Piece

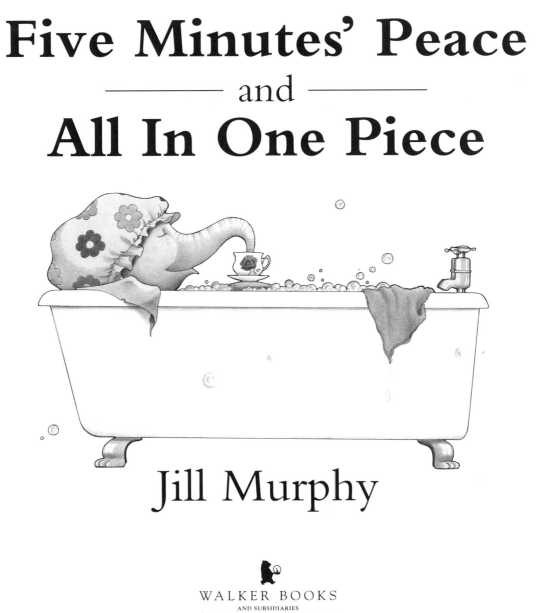

Jill Murphy

WALKER BOOKS
AND SUBSIDIARIES
LONDON · BOSTON · SYDNEY

First published as *Five Minutes' Peace* (1986)
and *All in One Piece* (1987)
by Walker Books Ltd
87 Vauxhall Walk, London SE11 5HJ

This edition published 1999

2 4 6 8 10 9 7 5 3 1

© 1986, 1987 Jill Murphy

Printed in Singapore

British Library Cataloguing in Publication Data
A catalogue record for this book is
available from the British Library.

ISBN 0-7445-7704-7

♪...with a little help from my friends.♪

For Geoff, Sue, Abby, Hannah, Nick & Polly, with love.

Five Minutes' Peace

The children were having breakfast.
This was not a pleasant sight.

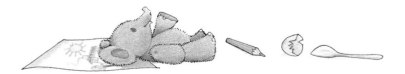

Mrs Large took a tray from the cupboard.
She set it with a teapot, a milk jug, her
favourite cup and saucer, a plate of
marmalade toast and a leftover cake
from yesterday. She stuffed the morning
paper into her pocket and sneaked off
towards the door.

"Where are you going with that tray, Mum?" asked Laura.

"To the bathroom," said Mrs Large.

"Why?" asked the other two children.

"Because I want five minutes' peace from *you* lot," said Mrs Large.

"That's why."

"Can *we* come?" asked Lester as they trailed
  up the stairs behind her.

"No," said Mrs Large, "you can't."

"What shall *we* do then?" asked Laura.

"You can play," said Mrs Large. "Downstairs.
  By yourselves. And keep an eye on the baby."

"I'm *not* a baby," muttered the little one.

Mrs Large ran a deep, hot bath.
She emptied half a bottle of bath-foam into
the water, plonked on her bath-hat and got in.
She poured herself a cup of tea and lay back
with her eyes closed.
It was heaven.

"Can I play you my tune?" asked Lester.

Mrs Large opened one eye. "Must you?" she asked.

"I've been practising," said Lester. "You told me to.

Can I? Please, just for *one* minute."

"Go *on* then," sighed Mrs Large.

So Lester played. He played "Twinkle, Twinkle,

Little Star" three and a half times.

In came Laura. "Can I read you a page from
my reading book?" she asked.

"*No*, Laura," said Mrs Large. "Go on, *all* of you,
off downstairs."

"You let Lester play his tune," said Laura.

"I heard. You like him better than me. It's not fair."

"Oh, don't be silly, Laura," said Mrs Large.

"Go *on* then. Just *one* page."

So Laura read. She read four and a half pages
of "Little Red Riding Hood".

In came the little one with a trunkful of toys.

"For *you*!" he beamed, flinging them all
   into the bath water.

"Thank you, dear," said Mrs Large weakly.

"Can I see the cartoons in the paper?" asked Laura.

"Can I have the cake?" asked Lester.

"Can I get in with you?" asked the little one.

Mrs Large groaned.

In the end they *all* got in. The
little one was in such a hurry that
he forgot to take off his pyjamas.

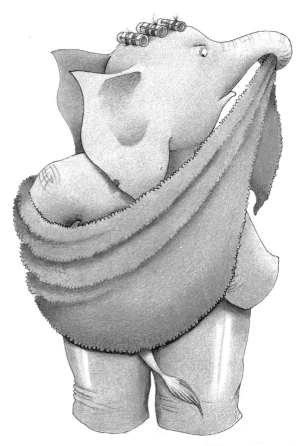

Mrs Large got out. She dried herself, put on her dressing-gown and headed for the door.

"Where are you going *now*, Mum?" asked Laura.

"To the kitchen," said Mrs Large.

"Why?" asked Lester.

"Because I want five minutes' peace from *you* lot," said Mrs Large.

"That's why."

And off she went downstairs, where she had three minutes and forty-five seconds of peace before they all came to join her.

All In One Piece

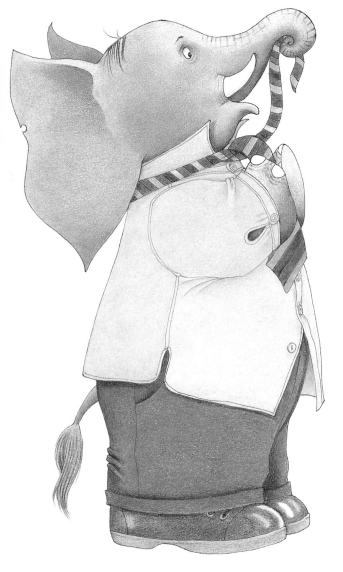

Mr Large was getting ready for work.
"Don't forget the office dinner-dance
tonight, dear," he said.
"Of course I won't," said Mrs Large.
"I've been thinking about it all year."

"Are children allowed at the dinner-dance?"
asked Lester.

"No," said Mrs Large. "It'll be too late
for little ones."

"What about the baby?" asked Luke.

"Granny is coming to take care of everyone,"
said Mrs Large, "so there's no need to worry."

Granny arrived at tea time. The children
were already bathed and in their nightclothes.
Granny gave them some painting to do while
she tidied up and Mr and Mrs Large went
upstairs to get ready.

Luke sneaked into the bathroom while
Mr Large was shaving.
"Will I have to shave when I grow up?"
he asked, patting foam onto his trunk.
"Go away," said Mr Large. "I don't want
you ruining my best trousers!"

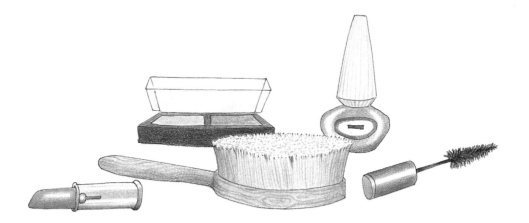

The baby crept into the bedroom where
Mrs Large was putting on her make-up.
Mrs Large didn't notice until it was too late.

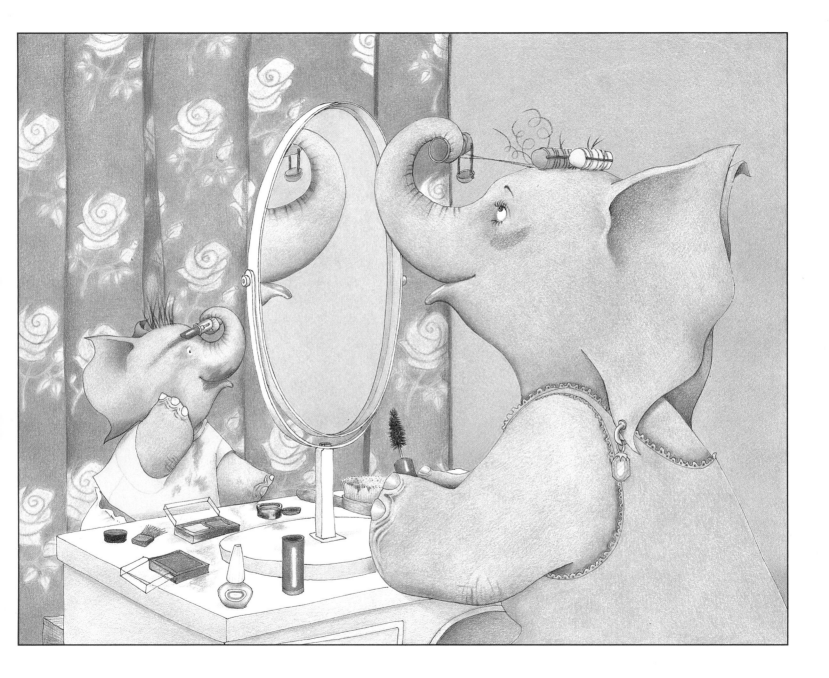

"Look!" said the baby. "Pretty!"

"Don't move," said Mrs Large. "Don't
touch *anything*!"

Outside on the landing, things were
even worse. Laura was clopping about in
her mother's best shoes and beads and
Lester and Luke were seeing how many
toys they could cram into her new tights.

"Downstairs at *once*!" bellowed Mrs Large.
"Can't I have just one night in the whole year
  to myself? One night when I am not covered in
  jam and poster-paint? One night when I can put
  on my new dress and walk through the front
  door all in one piece?"

The children went downstairs to Granny.
Mr Large followed soon after, very smart
in his best suit. At last, Mrs Large
appeared in the doorway.
"How do I look?" she asked.

"Pretty, Mummy!" gasped the children.

"What a smasher!" said Mr Large.

"You look like a film star, dear,"
  said Granny.

"Hands off!" said Mrs Large to the
  paint-smeared children.

Mr and Mrs Large got ready to leave.

"Goodbye everyone," they said. "Be good now."
 The baby began to cry.

"Just go," said Granny, picking her up.

"She'll stop as soon as you've left. Have a
  lovely time."

"We've escaped," said Mr Large with a smile,
closing the front door behind them.
"All in one piece," said Mrs Large, "and
not a smear of paint between us."
"Actually," said Mr Large gallantly, "you'd
look wonderful to me, even if you were
covered in paint."

Which was perfectly true ...
and just as well really!